A Kitten's Year

By Nancy Raines Day

Illustrated by Anne Mortimer

FRANCES LINCOLN

Text copyright © Nancy Raines Day 2000
Illustrations copyright © Anne Mortimer 2000

First published in Great Britain in 2000 by
Frances Lincoln Limited, 4 Torriano Mews,
Torriano Avenue, London NW5 2RZ

Published by arrangement with HarperCollins Publishers, New York

British Library Cataloguing in Publication Data available on request

ISBN 0-7112-1570-7

Printed in the USA

1 3 5 7 9 8 6 4 2

To my mother, Cecelia,
who nurtured my love of books
and endured my love of cats.
—N. R. D.

For Lesley
—A. M.

A kitten

peeks

at

January,

toys

with

February,

stalks

March,

paws

April,

tumbles

into

May,

leaps

at

June,

hides

from

July,

dozes

through

August,

chases September,

spooks
October,

sniffs
November,

dreams
December,

and wakes

up . . .

a cat.